...incess

By Sue Fliess · Illustrated by Natalie Smillie

🌹 A GOLDEN BOOK • NEW YORK

Text copyright © 2018 by Sue Fliess.
Cover art and interior illustrations copyright © 2018 by Natalie Smillie.
All rights reserved. Published in the United States by Golden Books, an imprint of Random House
Children's Books, a division of Penguin Random House LLC, 1745 Broadway,
New York, NY 10019, and in Canada by Penguin Random House Canada Limited, Toronto.
Golden Books, A Golden Book, A Little Golden Book, the G colophon, and the distinctive
gold spine are registered trademarks of Penguin Random House LLC.
rhcbooks.com
Educators and librarians, for a variety of teaching tools, visit us at
RHTeachersLibrarians.com
Library of Congress Control Number: 2017935533
ISBN 978-0-399-55642-5 (trade) — ISBN 978-0-399-55643-2 (ebook)
Printed in the United States of America
10 9 8 7 6 5 4 3 2 1

The royal marching band is here.
Soon the princess will appear!

I jump up so I can see
the royal princess wave to me!

"Over here! Please say hello!
Princess, how I love you so!"

"My name's Claire. How do you do?
May I ride up there with you?"

"Do come up! Sit by my side.
Look around. Enjoy the ride!"

"Will you teach me what you do?
Could *I* be a princess, too?"

"It's far trickier than it looks
or how it seems in storybooks."

"Don't you simply dress for tea
and feast with all the royalty?

"Maybe I don't
really know. . . ."

"Want a lesson? Quick—let's go!"

"Proper etiquette is key:
Please and *Thank you*.
Pardon me.

"Curtsy, nod, and stand up straight.

"Use your napkin.
Don't be late.

"Practice manners
when you're out.

"Speak with kindness.
Never shout."

"You must learn to greet a crowd—"

"Is being silly
still allowed?"

"Yes! I skateboard down the halls . . .

and boogie at the palace balls!"

"As a princess, use your grace
to make the world a better place.

"You'll take trips across the seas
and give your time to charities. . . ."

"Maybe I'll teach kids to read or spend some time with those in need."

"You have earned
    this special crown."

"Thank you!
    I won't let you down!"

"You'll be great—beyond compare.

"I now crown you . . .
PRINCESS CLAIRE!"